CW01086635

# A Dog Cat & Bird on My Mind

Jonathan A. Uko

ISBN: 979-8-9907731-0-3

# DEDICATION

I would like to dedicate this book to all the children and young people around the world as they continue their journey for learning and excitement.

# CONTENTS

# ACKNOWLEDGMENTS

I am extremely grateful to God for HIS grace and blessings in my life. I would like to thank my parents for their tireless support and unwavering love for me. I also want to express my gratitude to my friends, teachers and staff at Papplewick school who have welcomed and supported me over the past one and half years while schooling in the United Kingdom.

# 1 A DOG CAT AND BIRD ON MY MIND

A dog cat and bird on my mind
A happy end to the daily grind
I muster all the strength I can find
To remember if I've been kind
Despite covid homeless or blind.

Inspired now to share the joy
To serve or help a girl or boy
Many goodies O boy, O boy!
Bookmarks Cookies books for Roy
Issy, Liam, Walter, Troy.

Red, White and Blues
Colors and patriotic Hues
American and British flags are clues
Green Gradients give colorful cues
Mother Africa homage dues.

Dogs cats and birds each a different shape
All together make drawings people love to take
With Oatmeal raisin cookies I bake
Such joy flows smoothly like a lake.

**The End**

# 2 COUSINS AROUND THE WORLD

## THE STORY STARTS IN AMERICA
## IN THE BEAUTIFUL STATE OF PENNSYLVANIA....

There once lived a pentagon dog.
And his home was in a gooey bog.
He barked since there was, in the doghouse, an octagon cat he heard.
And he bellowed ferociously at the quadrilateral bird.

The dog's name was Penty.
The cat's name was Octy.
The bird's name was Quadril,
And this is the story that they tell.

At once, the dog named Penty,
Who rose out of the bog that is dirty,
Ran at Octy the cat,
While he yapped.

Quadril mocked Octy as, from a tree, he swooped down,
And Octy stared at Quadril with a frown.
Octy lunged gracefully,
But do not be deceived for he was angry.

So, the amazing Quadril,
Who is having a thrill,
Is being chased by Octy,
And who is close behind? Penty.

So, all with astonishing speed,
They chased each other, not realizing their greed.
From this, not realizing their haste,
They begin travelling all over the fifty states.

As they leave Pennsylvania,
They pass Maryland and enter the Virginias.
As they move on to Kentucky,
They pass on to Missouri.

As the non-stop animals make haste to Kansas,
They pass Oklahoma and move to Texas.
As they enter the sweltering heat,
They skip and dare not miss a beat.

They started to look for signs that told them
Where they had been chased about.
When one said Texas, they began to freak out.
But suddenly, they stopped realizing that it was not that bad,
Because in Texas, there were cousins that they had.

Quadril bit Octy's tail making him shout.
And from that Penty was startled and angry for Octy messing about.
And with that the animals that are silly, They travel to Houston, the biggest Texan city.
Since they were in Amarillo, they got chased to Laredo.
They then travelled to Waco and after, El Paso.
As they travelled along the Rio Grande,
All the way to the Island of South Padre.

From there they travelled to Galveston,
and finally, to Houston.
When they passed a big sign,
It said Houston, and they were not resigned.

They immediately went their separate ways.
To see if they could ask to stay with their cousins for some days.
Penty travelled to his cousin's bog, on the knoll,
Octy, the doghouse and Quadril, a tree that was tall.

Penty's cousin was a line doggy,
Octy's, a triangle kitty and Quadril's a circle birdy.
The doggy's name was Liney,
The kitty, Traily and Cirly the birdy.

After their fortnight of relaxing passed,
Penty, Octy and Quadril crossed paths.
They chased each other again into Mexico,
And into the whole of Central America, including Puerto Rico.

The obsessed animals got into South
America,
And travelled to Venezuela.
From there, to Guayana,
And then to Argentina.

With that, they travelled to Lima, Peru,
Once they found out got there, they stuck
together like glue.
Because they realize greatness in this
nation,
They remember aunty bear to their friend
Paddington.

With that, they raced to the house in the
tall trees,
Of Paddington's aunty Lucy's.
They asked if they could stay.
She agreed, only if they could obey.

And so, for a month, they obeyed.
When they left that lofty home, Aunt Lucy
was happy not dismayed.
As soon as they clambered down,
You guessed it! They turned things inside
out and upside-down.

They ran (and flew)
Across the Atlantic deep blue.
They ran over the waves,
Eventually, they saw an island far in their long
gaze.

Islands with green and pleasant land.
The name of it was England.
And, as if their luck were as bright and bold,
They arrived at the house of Danger Mouse,
DM, and Penfold.

They pleaded with DM "Do let us come in!",
And Penfold excited joined them welcoming.
Happy they shouted, "We are great fans!",
To which DM replied, "Man O Man!"

With reluctance, he allowed them to stay.
As they were cheering, there came the great
voice, it's Colonel K!
He said that they had to stop an attack,
That was planned by Stiletto and Baron
Greenback.

Penty, Octy and Quadril pleaded to help on the
mission.
And DM agreed again with resignation.
Penty, Octy and Quadril were distractions.
While DM and Penfold were for real actions.

Victorious, they got back, with hearty
congratulations, sent,
From Colonel K who made Penty, Octy and
Quadril honorary agents.
After celebrations and cheer,
They stayed for over half a year.

When it was time to leave, then,
The blessed animals got chased again.
They travelled through the countries of
Europe at steady speed.
Including the capital of Spain, Madrid.

Over the Black and Mediterranean Seas, they
ran,
Across to the country of Germany and
without a plan.
From there, they went to Serbia,
To travel to Bulgaria and Romania.

Onwards to the country of Ukraine.
From there, to Scotland, the highlands, and
plains.
Then they went to Ireland, the land of luck.
From there, they went to the Bourg of Lux.

Zip and zapping out of European Countries.
Zig and zagging they went to African
Mounties.
Now, they just noticed that they were on the
mountain of Kilimanjaro.
Lost and afraid, the animals began to weep in
deep sorrow.

But then, the trio realized something lucky.
They were just in time for the celebration of
South African rugby.
So, as Penty, Octy and Quadril raced to the
celebration,
Because there was a tight time slot to catch a
sensation.

They suggested what the South Africans could
do with the six million.
They suggested that they could buy more
homes with a billion.
And what did they do, pray tell you ask?
They chased each other. It's their only task.

They travelled from the island of Madagascar.
From there, they went to Nigeria.
They travelled next to Mali.
And then, raced to the DRC in a hurry.

From there they went to Namibia.
And on, to Somalia,
to Algeria,
And finally, to Ethiopia.

From Ethiopia to Mauritania.
Then, to Libya.
And finally, after travelling to Ghana,
Penty, Octy and Quadril finally stop in…
China?!

Their luck was incredibly bad,
For they were very sad.
For across the world, it was horrid,
Because there was the disease, Covid.

So, with that in mind, they had no time to
waste,
They went to a mask shop covering their noses
and mouths with haste.
They got some masks and went off to explore
Beijing,
Penty, Octy and Quadril trekked by foot and
enjoyed some biking.

They decided to eat some Chinese food for the
first time,
For this was going to be the best big time.
They started to try some Chinese food with the
chopsticks,
The food was good, but the chopsticks were
plastic.

Once these geometric animals were full of
food,
They were in a happy mood.
But, just then, as they exited the place,
They started to chase each other at a great pace.

First, they travelled to Russia, through ongoing
War,
Then, they went to Singapore.
Then, they went to Indonesia,
The Koreas, Malaysia, and India.

From there, Penty, Octy and Quadril went to
the countries with all the endings of "Stan,"
And after, they went to Iran.
From there, they went to Jordan,
And they went to Oman.

They went to Vietnam,
And then, to Taiwan.
Then, to Qatar,
And Cambodia.

From there this "Trig Trio", went to Armenia,
And from there, they went to Georgia.
From there, they went to Japan,
And then to Lebanon.

From there, they travelled to Sri Lanka,
And from there, on to Australia?!
They realized where they were because they
saw Uluru.
And they noticed that there was a tall
kangaroo!

They were spectating the kangaroos with
fascination.
With delight, it was a great revelation.
With that, they could not waste any time.
They chased each other before it was
nighttime.

They raced to Papua New Guinea
And from there, to Tonga.
From there, to Fiji,
And from there, to Kiribati.

From Kiribati to Nauru.
From Nauru to Tuvalu.
From Tuvalu to Palau,
From Palau to Niue.

From Niue to New Zealand,
From New Zealand to Norfolk Island.
From Norfolk Island to Samoa.
From Samoa, back to North America.

When they realized where they were, they
shouted with glee,
When they shouted with glee, they said,
"Yippee!"
Then, they stopped for a moment and not
being true gentlemen, with refrain,
They started to chase each other all over
again!

**The End**

7

# 3 THE WORLD OF SHAPES

There once was a dog that was made of heptagons,
A cat of circles and a bird of octagons.
They lived happily in Wisconsin, in the city of La Crosse,
But they always struggled to get across.

For there, across a long river with a strong tide
There was a town that was on the hither side.
At the La Crosse Riverside, near the fountain,
The water froze because it was as cold as a mountain.

The dog's name was Hepty,
The bird's name was Octy.
The cat's name was Circy,
And when they met, they were not happy.

They wanted to cross the icy, frigid river,
Across this state's border.
They wanted to get to the other side,
Because of the beach's frozen tide.

So, one by one, they ice skated gracefully on the ice.
They were having a time that was genuinely nice.
Eventually, after their great fun,
They reached the beach, in the cold sun.

They relaxed and brought their solar powered tanning stations.
This is to prevent the warming of globalization.
So, for an hour, they were getting tanned,
On the freezing, icy cold beach's sand.

Eventually, all the stations stopped,
Because the sun was blocked.
Unfortunately, it was snowing,
But they were already knowing.

They changed their solar stations to snow stations,
This was more of a solution than a situation.
So, they now were finishing their tans,
And they felt the cold like there were fans?

They opened the stations not knowing what happened,
For they have left the beach and the island.
Once they saw, they were moving,
Very quickly, not cruising.

While Hepty was panicking, he,
Saw a sign saying I90.
They had to stay on to not fall for sure,
So, Hepty said to Circy and Octy, "Please, close the door"!

So, they listened and closed those doors with a frown,
But they eventually slowed down.
They felt a big bump not knowing what was happening,
For they all heard some rattling.

But eventually,
It stopped unexpectedly,
Unfortunately,
After some effort, they opened their doors successfully.

Once they were opened, they had a great fall,
Not knowing where they are at all.
But then, they saw a sign that said, "This is the mall
For the twin city of Minneapolis, St Paul."

They were confused, not knowing where St Paul is,
So, they ignored it and hurried, for there was no time for showbiz.
After a couple of hours of trying to get their stations down,
They succeeded but were tired, so wore a frown.

They slept for eight hours in their tanning stations.
Once they woke up and opened the doors, they were in another nation.
For they, again, did not know where they are at all,
For the sign was gone and with it, the mall.

To prevent them from moving again,
They plodded upon the rugged terrain.
Eventually, they found a sign.
It was hard to read because it was nighttime.

With a deep sigh of rejection,
No wiser to the direction.
They could cast a lot,
And end up in Connecticut!

However, they made a warm camp.
With their snow stations, not a fire, or a
lamp.
Half an hour later, they slept in the
stations.
When they woke up, they felt a huge
sensation.

With a big bang from outside,
Their bodies were resting on the station's
side.
As they opened the doors with spirit,
They were incredulously shocked by the sound
of a bullet.

Hepty and Circy did not know where they were,
But Octy knew in a blur.
He said that this place was a place of guns,
rodeo and the "howdy" cowboy.
He was talking about Texas, the great state of
oil.
They were scared because of the guns,

Because they were not an object of fun.
They went back inside to protect themselves
from the bullets,
But after opening the doors half an hour later,
they were in the country of cricket.

Circy realized what was going on.
The solution was ringing like an airhorn.
She told Hepty and Octy her hypothesis,
And they tried it with incautiousness.

They closed the doors effortlessly,
And after five minutes, Octy's hypotheses
worked marvelously.
She realized that every time the door closed,
The station would travel to a different location,
so she proposed.

That once back in Wisconsin, they would take
the stations, solar or snow, to the junkyard.
Hepty and Octy agreed so they dumped them,
three stations crushed hard.
From these scraps, they built new non-place
travelling machines.
And had a wonderful time of their lives with the
past now blown to smithereens.


**The End**

# 4 AT THE SCHOOL OF PAPPLEWICK

At the school of Papplewick,
In September, there are new boys to take the "mic".
These boys are an Octagon Dog that was not absurd,
An unwavering Line Cat and a regular Pentagon Bird.

The dog is named Octy,
The cat is called Liney, and the bird Penty.
They want to play some football,
So, they went off to find the great hall.

But someone told them "That's the wrong direction!",
So, showed them the way with no objection.
Once they got there, the instructor asked, "Why are you late?"
They said, "We don't know!", so began a big debate.

Once that was over, they played in teams.
With great teammates, to win, it is easier than it seems.
Both teams ended up with an equalizer.
Afterward, they have a delicious appetizer.

This went on for every day of the week, except Wednesday and Saturday.
This is because they have matches against other schools, at home, or away.
They win some of the matches, but they also lose some.
They also drew some matches, but altogether, it was exceptionally fun.

For PE, they played basketball and badminton (which is much like tennis).
The games are such fun, they wish that they were endless!
They played them every day during the football season.
They really liked to play basketball and badminton in the region.

After the football season is over, they are incredulously sad,
Because the fun is over, they are also very mad.
However, their mood changed thankfully,
Because they are playing rugby, which they agreed to exceptionally.

They have fun playing rugby tackling one another,
And when they run, each an un-stopper.
When they score "trys", they celebrate gratefully,
And when they "tackle", they make sure to do it carefully.

When it is time for matches, they do exceptionally well again.
They have their draws, losses, and wins which they can sustain.
They play like in real rugby matches.
They play in fifteens and once they get the ball, they make dashes.

They have fun, but some matches are cancelled,
Because the pitches get frozen, it could hurt when you get tackled.
Other days, the pitches are very muddy,
So, when you run fast with studs, it would make the pitches look ugly.

For PE, they play hockey that is not on the ice.
For them, without ice is exceptionally nice.
They use hockey pucks and hockey sticks.
A great "WHACK" into the goals protected by goalie using special tricks.

After rugby, it's off to cricket, so, thinking it is baseball,
Liney, Octy and Penty put their caps sideways, trying to show them all
That they were playing an American sport,
So, the instructor sighs and decides to sort.

By showing them what cricket is and how to play it.
They see what cricket is and how it could hurt People, Liney, Octy and Penty if hit by the cricket ball. They see how different it is to a baseball's ball.

The whole cricket sport is similar as well.
Liney, Octy and Penty think that this is some sort of crazy spell.
The wickets are the umpires, and the bases.
So, the bowler throws the ball to hit the wicket, so the batter has the paces.

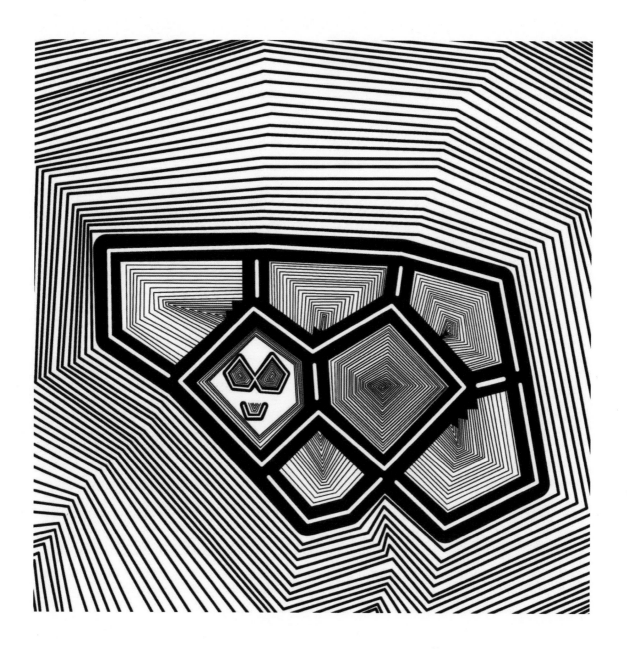

Another way to get out is for someone to
"catch" it.
The grounds are filled with rough grit.
The bat for cricket is surprisingly flat,
While for baseball, it is a rotundly bat.

Anyway, enough about the sport similarities.
Let's talk about the sport strategies.
The way to win the game is that you must hit the
ball both hard and far.
You also must be pacy to be "The Star".

So, during the season, there are mostly wins,
Very few losses, and some draws with grins.
During the cricket season, Liney, Octy and Penty
must compete in athletics.
They were relieved because they thought they had
to do gymnastics!

Octy did the hundred-meter-dash while Liney did
the high-jump.
Penty did shotput and the ball went down with a
big "Thump!".
For PE, they had to play tennis which is
exhilarating.
They say they "love" tennis, they aren't
exaggerating.

Once the cricket season is over, they must prepare
again for the football season.
They like football, so they stay and play football for
that reason.
Before the start of school football, Papplewick has
Stag Camp,
They are so excited their emotions glow like a lamp!

**The End**

## 5 MY OHIO THE GREAT

Eons ago, in the great US State of Ohio,
There were three animals who do not have
enormous egos.
The dog has heptagons; the bird has lines
The cat has quadrilaterals, and they all have an
enjoyable time.

Hepty is the dog's name, and the cat is called Quad,
The bird is called Liney and when they saw each
other, they were like a military squad.
They are in the city of Cleveland
With Lake Eyrie this City of Light, they lived on the
shoreland.

One bright day, they saw each other, and their
differences, but surprisingly,
They did not get mad at each other, outstandingly.
In fact, they decided not to fight at all that day.
This cool trio decided to visit places in Ohio, so
they went together, on their merry way.

First stop is to Lake Eyrie for a quick swim in the
freezing cold.
However, the animals' minds must have been
incredulously bold!
After their freezing bath, they shook the water off,
And decided to take another activity for their fun
day off.

They agreed to go to the popular Cincinnati
Amusement Park.
To the thrilling roller coaster, where Hepty made a
hefty bark!
On the nail-biting water slide, Quad made a shrill
meow.
At the loud shooting game, Liney shouts "MOVE
ON NOW"!

Onwards to the impressive sports arena Rocket
Mortgage Fieldhouse,
Where they decided to watch as quiet as a mouse.
They saw "The King" LeBron James play at a
game,
This was where he got his wonderful fame.

The Cavaliers won, so everyone celebrated.
Even Penty, Quad and Liney joined in with the
fascinated
Crowd and even stood and shouted "We love
You Cavaliers" from their seats from above.

This trio decided to cheer all other Ohioan
teams.
And made incredulously loud screams!
First in line are the Akron Rubber Ducks who
play baseball.
Then, to Cincinnati Bengals for "All
American" fast paced football.

With the Cincinnati Cyclones it is time for
impressive hockey.
Cleveland Browns afterward for football at
the stadium of First Energy.
Later to the Cleveland Charge for fun
basketball for the League of G
Via Cleveland Monsters and Columbus Blue
Jackets for more exciting hockey.

Forward to Columbus Clippers for some
hardy baseball.
Next, it's Columbus Crew SC for beautiful
soccer in a great hall.
Then rugged Dayton Dragons for more
baseball, it's the Midwest League,
And more soccer with FC Cincinnati with
friends and a colleague.

Lake County Captains is next for their brawny
baseball in Eastlake Ohio,
And tough Toledo Mud Hens' baseball in
Toledo
Then, to the Toledo Walleye,
With a stop at Youngstown, both for some
thrilling hockey.

Now cheering completed, visits are done and
already it's nightfall.
So back to Cleveland for some sleep and a
parting round of football.
Each to bed, they slept and slept and soon it
was the morning,
They crossed paths again, their truce now
broken, and gave each other a warning!

**The End**

## 6 SHAPE-O-WICK

Deep in the woods in Berkshire is a remarkable school called Shape-O-wick,
Three animals exist who sing simply terrific.
One animal is a bass-tenor, a circle dog called Circy.
Cat is made up of Pentagons, named Penty and thinks alto is quite easy.

Treble-soprano bird makes the trio complete, made of lines, he is called Liney.
The jolly friends are in a school choir where they had to sing only
Fifteen sopranos with Liney, five altos with Penty.
And ten bass-tenors with Circy. New to the choir, the three were anxious really.

Their first song, they sung as canaries which surprised the school choir
So, nervousness was now down to the wire.
On Saturday the trio's first time,
So beautiful was the music parents clapped at their magnificent chime.

When the head of the choir announced that they were going to Cloistershire for the first time,
The animals, excited, celebrated because they knew it would be sublime!
After the session was over, the trio left to pack for the trip.
Thrilled to the core, they knew that they must not slip!

As excellent singers, they said to each other "No need to practice"
But teacher heard and warned instead "It's practice for all including each novice"
Time to leave on the choir trip, everyone brought suitcases to the coach.
Bags here, boxes there no space for even a roach!

When on the road, they sang songs for an hour out of three, then everybody slept.
Arrived at the abbey, and went to sing except
One of the choir shapes, was incredibly sick.
So, as a team they sang out loud at the abbey and it turned out pretty slick.

Recital completely over, everyone clapped and some cheered.
And the choir was relieved because they thought some people sneered.
After all that singing workout and stress,
An exquisite meal awaits at the yummy pizza restaurant called "Pizza Shape Express".

Mealtime now over, the choir took the coach to the hotel, "First Shape Inn."
With pizzas and a five-star hotel, it was a win-win.
Nighttime came then daytime and another excellent meal,
Then time to go, the animal trio had another squeal.

Why? Because there were these little gnomes, they were all called Gonks.
Meant to be for good luck for shapes who had head bonks.
At Evensong the choir sung with some parents as the audience.
All done Circy, Penty & Liney bought curios at the quaint store with great diligence.

After that riveting performance, the choir left and went to Shape-O-Donalds,
Some shapes ordered burgers; some chose nuggets all accompanied by the adults.
They also had some store games to play which were so much fun.
Only two games that were played required the players to run.

Shape-O-Donalds done, the choir went on to a serious service.
So, everyone was incredibly studious on the premises.
With seriousness over, they went to a place which was not gross.
They went to the one, the only, Nando's!

Everyone had their meal with chicken and with sauce.
Some meals were longer than others, but eventually came with the shapes' voices hoarse,
From shouting to the waiters "we are hungry, please hurry up!"
The food arrived and they were happy, at least they got the grub.

Nando's adventure now over, they travelled to another "First Shape Inn."
Excited still in unbelief the shapes asked, "pinch my skin!"
It's off to bed, then early wake, Circy, Penty & Liney off to hearty breakfast,
Now back to school, to Shape-O-wick, to parents – it's been such a blast!

**The End**

## 7 LA CROSSE ADVENTURE

In a town called La Crosse, Wisconsin,
There were three animals, but do not make a
quick assumption.
A dog made of quads, a cat made of hexagons,
And a bird made of quaxagons. The trio were a
family with acceptance.

The word, quaxagons is a mixture between quads
and hexagons, you see.
And, after this sentence, you will be especially
happy.
The dog, Quad, and the cat, Hex, are married and
have a young son, the bird, Quadex.
They were a happy family, but Quadex had a
super-fast reflex.

Whenever he flew, he could do it at the speed of
jets, but he could also fly at normal speed.
He was from an extremely rare breed.
He was the last of his kind.
A scientist told the couple that finding that bird
was incredulously impossible to find.

One beautiful, sunny day, the trio went to see
some landmarks.
Some of them had famous monarchs.
There was one statue with a Native American
Chief at River Side Park.
When the trio saw it, they gave a loud chirp,
meow, and bark.

Next was a large, steel eagle demonstrating
freedom on the road circle.
It looks big from up close, but from far away, the
statue's appearance is little.
As they moved on to the fountain and the ground
showed different nearby towns.
Trempealeau, Onalaska, Winona were such
remarkable nouns!

Once Riverside Park was done, they went over to
visit the Charmont Hotel.
It looked like a factory on the outside, but on the
inside, it was not a motel.
They had an exquisite brunch at Charmont, then
they decided to leave Fairfield hotel
Which was next to the Blue Bridge which people
might want to dwell.

They travelled to Gundersen Health, the main
hospital around this area.
With branches in the twin town, Onalaska, and
Gundersen, Winona.
The Distillery is where they went next and ate
some dinner.
In summer, there are rows of tables on a
wooden platform on the road unlike in winter.

The food was such a delight, and, in the
window, there was a brewing system.
Qaudex was curious, so his wise parents
explained with their smart wisdom.
Once dinner was done, the trio travelled back to
Charmont to pack, for they were travelling.
Tomorrow, to England with a connecting flight
and, on a flight, Quadex was journaling

His day first started with the two statues,
But he wondered who made and structured the
statues and who was the native's muse.
Then, he wrote about Gundersen and talked
about its branches.
And, just as he was about to write his brunch at
Charmont, there were sudden bashes.

This happened because the plane landed on the
runway in England.
When Quadex looked out the window, the fog
outside had really thickened.
Quadex woke up his parents, and said "O look,
we are back in the UK!".
Quad and Hex looked at each other, and
laughed because England was known for its
showers and spray.

**The End**

# ABOUT THE AUTHOR

My name is Jonathan and I love writing poems featuring digital Dog Cat and Bird characters which I create to inspire others. I started drawing Dogs Cats and Birds in my journal, for fun, during the COVID lock down and now I want to inspire others to be creative. My mum and my dad support me in my business. Enjoy the poems and subscribe on my website www.dogcatandbirdmedia.com for more updates.

Printed in Great Britain
by Amazon